I0817009

HOW TO DEAL

Developing Skills for Coping

by Ben Hubbard

CAPSTONE PRESS
a capstone imprint

Capstone Captivate is published by Capstone Press, an imprint of Capstone.
1710 Roe Crest Drive
North Mankato, Minnesota 56003
www.capstonepub.com

Library of Congress Cataloging-in-Publication Data

Names: Hubbard, Ben, 1973- author.
Title: How to deal : developing skills for coping / Ben Hubbard.
Description: North Mankato, Minnesota : Capstone Press, an imprint of Capstone, [2021] | Series: Chill | Includes bibliographical references and index. | Audience: Ages 8-11 | Audience: Grades 4-6 | Summary: "Nerves. Stress. Life spiraling out of control. Things that cause anxiety are all around. That's completely normal! The good news is that we can all learn how to deal with those feelings in a healthier, more effective way. Find out what you can do to cope with any problem that comes at you"-- Provided by publisher. Identifiers: LCCN 2020044486 (print) | LCCN 2020044487 (ebook) | ISBN 9781496695215 (hardcover) | ISBN 9781977154408 (pdf) | ISBN 9781977156075 (kindle edition)
Subjects: LCSH: Stress (Psychology)--Juvenile literature. | Adjustment (Psychology)--Juvenile literature.
Classification: LCC BF575.S75 H828 2021 (print) | LCC BF575.S75 (ebook) | DDC 155.9/042--dc23
LC record available at https://lccn.loc.gov/2020044486
LC ebook record available at https://lccn.loc.gov/202004448

Image Credits
Capstone Studio: Karon Dubke, 13; iStockphoto: Steven_Kriemadis, 6; Shutterstock: antoniodiaz, 22 top, ArtVisionStudio, 10, Backgroundy, 21, Bestujeva_Sofya, design element, cidepix, design element, Darren Baker, cover, 1, ESB Professional, 19, Fernando Avendano, 20 left, Flas100, design element, Laia Design Lab, 7 top, LightField Studios, 20 right, Monkey Business Images, 24, 26, 27, pimchawee, 5, Plasteed, design element, Pressmaster, 29, Rawpixel.com, 22 bottom, SergiyN, 9, sirtravelalot, 8, stockyimages, 14, 15, svtdesign, 12, Tom Wang, 4, Torychemistry, 11, wavebreakmedia, 17, woocat, 16, Yayayoyo, 25, Yeti Crab, 23, 28

Editorial Credits
Editors: Mari Bolte and Alison Deering; Designers: Juliette Peters and Sarah Bennett; Media Researchers: Jo Miller and Tracy Cummins; Production Specialist: Laura Manthe

All internet sites appearing in back matter were available and accurate when this book was sent to press.

Printed in the United States 4999

Table of Contents

Words in **bold** are in the glossary.

Introduction

Are You Coping?

Do you ever get **anxious** or nervous? Does life sometimes stress you out? Have you found yourself worrying about things beyond your control? Are there times when everything piles up around you? Do you ever feel like you simply can't **cope**?

If the answer is "yes," then relax. "Yes" is everyone's answer! All of us have felt like we have failed to cope at some point in our lives. It is a normal and natural part of being human. The good news is that we can all learn to become better at coping.

Action Versus Emotions

Learning to cope involves two things:

- taking action to manage your problems
- managing the way you feel about your problems

The toughest thing to accept is that some things can't be changed. But you can work toward changing the way you feel about those things.

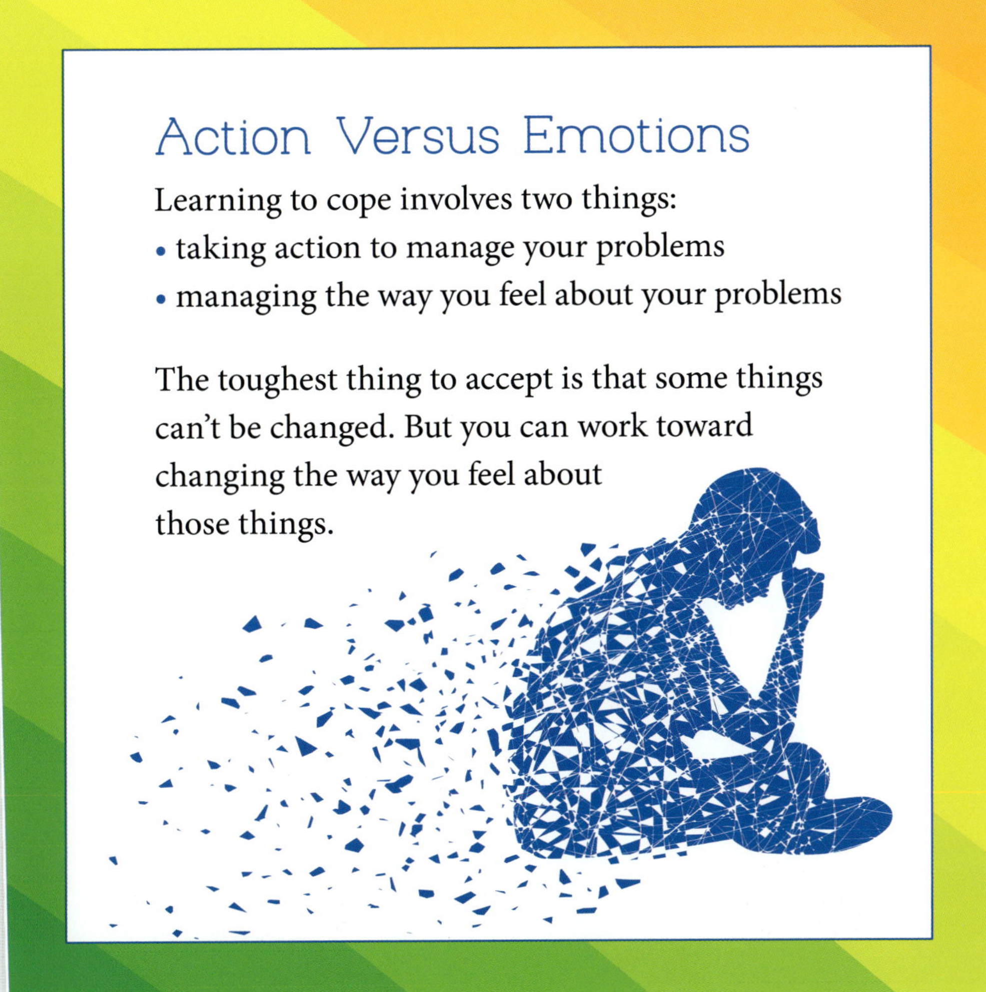

Chapter 1

Busy Lives

The modern world is a fast-paced place. We're busier than ever with school, homework, chores, extracurricular activities, and family events. There never seems to be enough time to do everything. Stack on the pressure to succeed, from doing well on tests to being the best at sports. Does it ever feel like it's just too much?

Break it Down

Take a deep breath. Can you feel those **commitments** weighing you down? You can't get rid of them completely, but you can break the load into smaller, more manageable chunks. Grab a pen and paper. Set them by your bed. Every morning, make a to-do list. Set a realistic time frame for each task. When you've finished that task, cross it off your list. Don't worry about the things that aren't on your list. If they were important, they would be there. *You* are in control, not your commitments.

DO TODAY

1. finish reading chapter 2
2. unload and load dishwasher
3. practice piano
4. fold and put away laundry

Trauma and Trouble

Bad things happen. They happen to everyone. Accidents, illnesses, or money problems are things that happen and can't be controlled. They can bring great anxiety and stress to your life. But it is possible to get through these tough times.

Dealing with Death

When someone close to you dies, it is natural to feel sad. You may also feel guilt or angry at yourself—"I should have spent more time with that person!" or, "What if I could have done something differently?" Don't keep your feelings to yourself. Talking to someone who knew the person that died can help you deal with personal loss.

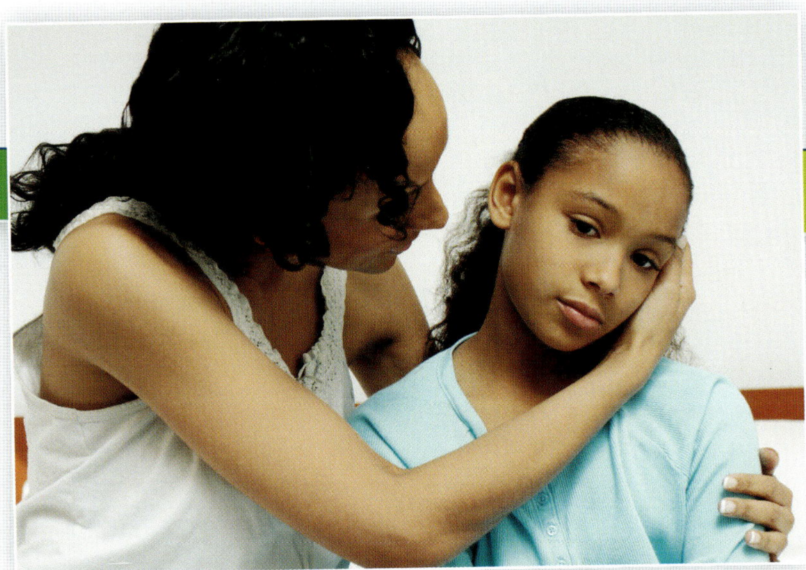

The Importance of People

Phone a friend! Everyone goes through tough times. Finding someone to talk to is a great way to release some of the pressure you feel. And there are so many different ways to communicate. Whether you talk, text, video chat, message, e-mail, or find a place to be anonymous online, there are outlets. It's not good to keep things bottled up inside.

Chapter 2

Get Calm to Cope

Stress is unhealthy. Stress makes us tense our bodies, clench our jaws, and breathe rapidly. If you're constantly stressed, it can actually have long-term effects on your body. Panic or anxiety attacks can make things worse. Calm down before things get too bad. Try balloon breathing when you need to calm down quickly.

Balloon Breathing

Place your hands on your stomach.

Pretend there is a balloon in your stomach that blows up each time you breathe in.

Inhale slowly and feel the balloon inflating.

Exhale slowly and feel the balloon deflating.

Repeat the exercise for at least two minutes.

The Power of Breathing

When you're stressed, you may have a "fight-or-flight" response. Your body is ready for **imminent** danger, such as an attack. You may panic, or you may lash out. It's time to relax. Do some deep breathing. This triggers a "relaxation" response. It lowers the body's heartbeat and encourages calmness. Being calm helps when coping with difficult situations.

Ask for Help

One big thing to remember is that everyone needs help coping with aspects of their life from time to time. Everyone! Someone else is probably going through the same thing you are. Don't be afraid to ask for help. You may even help each other come up with a solution.

Who to Ask?

It can be hard to open up. Who can you trust? Who will give good advice without judging? Friends or siblings are the easiest option. You could talk to an older family member, such as a parent, guardian, aunt, or uncle. A teacher, guidance counselor, or social worker can be a helpful person outside of your immediate circle. There are also call-in help lines if you want to talk to someone you don't know.

Chapter 3

Learning to Cope

When there are too many things to do and not enough time to do them, small changes can seem enormous. The addition of a test or an extra homework assignment can make your load unbearable. You may want to scream or slam a door. You may want to give up. You may want to throw everything in the air and walk away. Don't let the stress win! Take control by managing your activities.

Identify and Organize

Manage your activities by organizing them into groups. Here's how:

1. Draw four columns on a piece of paper with the headings:

Need to Do	Don't Need to Do	Enjoy	Don't Enjoy

2. Fill the columns with your weekly activities.

3. Look at the columns. Can you stop doing some of the Don't Need to Do or Don't Enjoy activities? Can they wait for another, less busy time? If the answer is yes, erase them.

4. Look at the activities that are still on the chart. Give each a time amount and assign a day to do it. Write this into a weekly schedule.

5. Always leave time to do things you enjoy. Otherwise, life becomes dull!

Stuck with a Situation

Sometimes a problem never seems to go away. Day after day it's the same old thing. Bullying, not getting enough sleep, or spending too much time online are common issues. You could shrug, say, "That's just how it is," and try to work around it. But ignoring a problem often makes things worse. Find a way to fix or get rid of your problem instead.

Break the Cycle

Many of us spend too much time on our phones, laptops, and gaming consoles. Sometimes we can even get **addicted**. That addiction can lead to poor sleeping habits too. To break the cycle, try a digital **detox**. Put your electronic devices away for a week. You'll be amazed by how much time you free up.

Finding Help

Did you know that serious issues like bullying or trolling are actually crimes? Your state has anti-bullying laws. If you're being bullied, don't just brush it off. Talk to an adult, such as a parent or a teacher. Any form of emotional or physical abuse, whether it's at school or at home, makes coping difficult or even impossible.

Become a Problem Solver

How do you cope with a problem? By tackling it! Start by writing down what's bothering you. Then come up with five possible solutions for each problem. Decide which of them you will try and when to put them into action. Is there a pattern to how you solve each problem? Just having a plan should help you feel better.

I don't understand my homework.

Fill in the answers with numbers just to finish it.

Re-read the instructions and try again.

Ask mom for help.

Text a friend to get the answers.

Talk to my teacher about it in class tomorrow.

Positive Thinking

There are a billion problems in the world. You can't solve them all. But you can try to control how you feel about those problems. Think about how you describe a problem to yourself. Then flip it on its head. Instead of thinking, "Everyone knows that I didn't do well on the test. . . . They're laughing at me. . . . I'm a failure," think, "Nobody knows what score I got. . . . I did get some questions right. . . . If I study harder I'll do better next time." It may sound corny, but self-confidence can do wonders!

Chapter 4

Coping Strategies

You've solved one problem. On to the next! Finding solutions to problems can be fun (especially when it works out well)! Problems aren't the only things that need solving, though. What about future goals? What do you want to do to make your life better? Do you want to spend more time with an elderly relative? Take up a new sport? Learn to draw? Be realistic about what you can achieve, but don't be scared of failure. You can do anything!

Positive Self-Belief

When you solve your problems and set achievable goals, you're also building your self-confidence. When you're self-confident, you stand taller and straighter. People will notice!

You can boost your self-confidence even when things are not going well. Find five things you like about yourself. Say them to yourself every day. Positive **affirmations** are a reminder of personal strengths and abilities. (You're great, by the way!)

Don't be Scared of Failure

That feeling of failure when you don't do something well is universal. Sometimes you feel like you fail at many things. But how you feel doesn't reflect who you are. Trying and failing is better than not trying at all. Failing at something is also a great teacher. It shows you what to do differently next time. Getting back up after failing and trying again is the most important thing.

A Famous Failure

Some of the most important people from history failed—and failed often. One example is Thomas Edison, the inventor of the lightbulb. Edison tried unsuccessfully to market an electric pen, a talking doll, concrete houses, and tinfoil records. When asked about his many failures, Edison replied, "I have not failed 10,000 times—I've successfully found 10,000 ways that will not work."

Do Away with Worry

That feeling of anxiety that eats away at you when you are worried is natural. You might be worried about being rejected by your friends or failing a test. To protect yourself, you may avoid certain situations or ask others to constantly reassure you. Unfortunately, nobody can control bad things from happening. Don't let that worry you further, though. Worry is the thing that we can control.

Where's the Proof?

Worry is like a little voice telling us, "Watch out! Bad things are coming!" But worry never shows us the proof. Worry never tells us that most things actually work out for the best. Did you know you can manage worry? You can talk back to the little worry voice by saying, "Where's the proof that will happen?" or, "You said that before, but nothing came of it." This will help stop worrying from becoming a bad habit.

Where's the proof?

You said that before, but nothing came of it!

Change Your Environment

Feeling trapped or stuck is another reaction when you are not coping. Sometimes we become stuck thinking obsessively about a problem. Other times, we might feel chained to our desks. Look around. Are you feeling moody or **indifferent**? This is a good time to change your environment.

Changing your environment for a few hours can help for two reasons: First, it can take you away from your everyday problems. Second, it can show you that there is a big world outside full of possibilities. Doing something physical, such as running or playing with friends, can be a great boost. You can also try something more challenging.

A New Challenge

Trying a new form of physical exercise is a great way to challenge yourself and boost your self-confidence. Afterward, you'll feel ready to take on the world. Ask your parents to help you choose something. Here are some suggestions:

swimming

yoga

rock climbing

mountain biking

jogging

gymnastics

a team sport you haven't tried before

Reflecting Back

After reading this book, do you feel better able to cope with your problems? Did you identify the things troubling you? Did you form a plan of action to tackle them? The final step is to **reflect** on how your plan went. To do this, write four headings on a piece of paper:

Problem	Plan	Suggested Solution	Outcome

Now fill in the blank spaces below the headings.

Future Learning

The purpose of the exercise is to remember how you felt about a problem and the process you put in place to solve it. Maybe it didn't work at first (remember Thomas Edison?) and that is OK. Hopefully you found a solution in the end. But did trying to tackle your problem make you feel different about yourself? Every time you try is a step closer to being better at coping.

Glossary

addiction (uh-DIK-shun)—a dependence on a drug, thing, or activity

affirmation (af-er-MEY-shuhn)—an act of saying or showing that something is true

anxiety (ang-ZYE-uh-tee)—a feeling of worry or fear

commitment (kuh-MIT-mihnt)—a promise to do something

cope (KOHP)—deal successfully with something difficult

detox (DEE-tahks)—going without a particular substance or activity

imminent (IM-uh-nuhnt)—about to happen

indifferent (in-DIFF-uh-ruhnt)—having no particular interest

reflect (ri-FLEKT)—to think back on

Read More

Andrus, Aubre and Karen Bluth. *Me Time: How to Manage a Busy Life*. North Mankato, MN: Capstone Press, 2018.

Chansard, Tabatha. *Conquer Anxiety Workbook for Teens: Find Peace from Worry, Panic, Fear, and Phobias*. Emeryville, California: Althea Press, 2019.

Sockolov, Matthew. *Practicing Mindfulness: 75 Essential Meditations to Reduce Stress, Improve Mental Health, and Find Peace in the Everyday*. Emeryville, California: Althea Press, 2018.

Internet Sites

ACTIVEkids: 13 Stress Relief Tips for Kids
activekids.com/parenting-and-family/articles/13-stress-relief-tips-for-kids

Coping Skills for Kids: Calming Anxiety in Children
copingskillsforkids.com/calming-anxiety

Coping Skills for Kids: Handling Stress
copingskillsforkids.com/how-to-deal-with-stress

Index